Dedicated to **Salman** and **Zayan**

It was a boring day at Dubai zoo,

It was closed for national day, so there was

nothing to do.

No chatter, no music, no fun and no noise.

No visitors, no children, no games and no toys.

"I'm lonely," Lion said with a sorrowful moan.

"It's a lovely day but we're left all on our own!"

Then **Zebra** had an idea! He got
up and he said,
"I'm tired of lazing, spending the
whole day in bed."

"Since no one's come to visit and
today's been a bore,
let's take the day off and go out
and **explore** !"

"The weather is perfect; the sun is so bright,
let's sightsee all day, and we'll stay out all night!"

"So come on everyone, it's UAE day!
Why waste our time? Let's go out and PLAY!"

The animals shouted
"Yippee! Woohoo!!!
Let's discover **Dubai** !
What's the first thing we'll
do?!"

"I have a idea,' said Giraffe,
"you'll like it, I hope,
lets go to **Mall of
emirates** to slide
down the ski slope!"

"We can sip hot cocoa at
St. Moritz Cafe ,
then lunch at the food
court! So...what do you
say?"

The **animals** ate, shopped and played.

Then they hurried downtown where they saw the **parade** .

They watched the **water fountains** dance as they stood outside.

Then they went to **GLOBAL VILLAGE** and sat on all the rides.

They snacked on **shawarmas** which were simply delish.

Then they went to **Dubai MALL** to see all the fish.

"What next?" asked Giraffe,

"what else can we see?

How about going for a ride on a

desert safari?"

"Then after that, before it gets too dark,
let's see the sunset from Atlantis Waterpark ."

Later that night the animals climbed up so high,
to see the stars from Burj Khalifa against the
moonlit sky.

They felt so lucky to live in this city, it's so vibrant and fun.
Where there's **energy** and **culture**

How about **YOU**? Have you done/seen these **things** yet?

Have you been to **Ripe Market**?

Have you ever had **henna** designs applied on your hands?

Have you ever been on an **abra** ride?

Have you ever eaten a yummy **iftar** in Ramadan?

Have you visited the **Gold Souk**?

Have you ever gone to **Art Dubai**?